This book belongs to

- -

For Louise

First published in **April 2022** by Haynes Mear Communications Ltd
Registered office: 7 White Hill Road, Barton-Le-Clay, Bedfordshire MK45 4PF.
Trading office: 49 Fir Tree Close, Flitwick, Bedfordshire MK45 1NY.
www.haynesmear.com

Written by **Carrie Knight**
All illustrations by **Lily Steel**
Giraffes On Tour branding by Haynes Mear Communications Ltd
& 'Geoffrey' animated character by digital illustrator Berni Georges
Book design / layout by **Clive Mear**

ISBN 979-8-8040-2636-4
Amazon KDP Distribution version

www.giraffesontour.co.uk   www.gosh.org

Never Alone features and thanks:

Royal Air Force Typhoon Display Team
Geoffrey has flown with Flight Lieutenant James Sainty, the
British Typhoon Display Pilot.

The Red Arrows
The Red Arrows took Geoffrey along on their flypast to help celebrate
RAF Mildenhall's 90th birthday.

U-2
Giraffes on Tour shot to the highest heights, speeding Geoffrey to the edge of space,
in reconnaissance aircraft 'Dragon Lady'.

HMS Queen Elizabeth
A giraffe at sea? Yes! Geoffrey hit the high seas, travelling the world during
the 7 months of HMS QE's maiden deployment.

The NHS Spitfire Project
Remembered forever. Geoffrey's name is written on the NHS Spitfire,
alongside his best friend Louise and their family.

Written by Carrie Knight

Illustrated by Lily Steel

Geoffrey Giraffe was exceedingly tall;

So tall he could look from the ground and see all.

But when he looked 'round from the skies to the floor,

He knew in his heart that he wanted much more.

As he sat by himself and looked up to the sky,
Dismayed and disheartened, he let out a sigh.

"I want a companion, a friend, and a chum;

A reason to love and be happy, not glum."

Then a voice on the wind,
sounding young and carefree,

Spoke to Geoffrey so sweetly:

"Share adventures with me."

So, suddenly curious,

he surveyed all around,

When a shadow above brought

an ear-splitting sound.

The roar of jet engines could not be mistaken,

As Geoffrey's excitement

began to awaken.

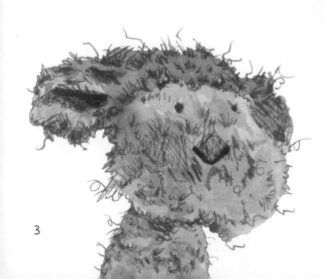

"A flight in a jet would be fun!"
Geoffrey reckoned.

As the pilot got out and over, he beckoned.

"A giraffe for a friend, would be great!" was his cry.

"Geoffrey, please come with me, when I fly."

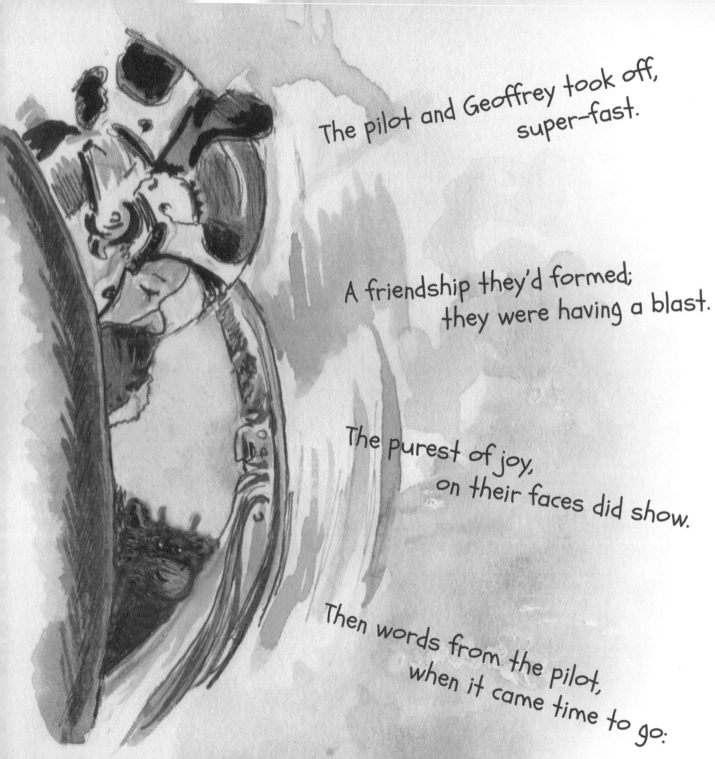

The pilot and Geoffrey took off,
super-fast.

A friendship they'd formed;
they were having a blast.

The purest of joy,
on their faces did show.

Then words from the pilot,
when it came time to go:

5

"Blue skies to you Geoffrey, wherever you are.
Blue skies to you Geoffrey, when you go, near or far.
Fly safe on your travels, search high and search low.
Fly safe on your journey and mind how you go."

Then a voice on the breeze,
                    that was happy and free,

Spoke to Geoffrey so kindly:

"Let's fly, you and me!"

6

Onwards he travelled,
to search for much more.

Looking for something
to love and adore.

Then, a roar louder,
than just from one jet.
And ribbons above
he could not forget.

Not one, but NINE planes came in over his head,
And came to a stop, on the ground up ahead.

They landed in front of all four of his feet.
Nine pilots he ran to, to chat to and greet.

"Geoffrey, come fly with us and Red 10. Together we'll loop up and over again."

Geoffrey jumped into
the jet from the floor.

Then shrieked with excitement
with what was in store.

The joyous gymnastics
they did in the sky,
made Geoffrey so happy,
he felt he could cry.
The pilots had brought to
him – friendship and fun,
though their message to
him had not yet begun.

"Good day to you Geoffrey, as you look to the sky.
Good day to you Geoffrey. Fly free and fly high.
Enjoy all your travels. Take-in everything.
Enjoy every journey and all that they bring."

Then, a voice on the thermals, with kindness and grace,
Spoke to Geoffrey sincerely:

"Come with me, to space."

As he looked to the sky, white clouds now had gone,
where darkness that came where the sun once had shone.

A roaring behind
brought the lights
of a plane, and a
fluttering feeling
he could not explain.

The pilot stepped out
	and greeted him now.
Geoffrey was wowed;
	so he graced with a bow.

The pilot was wearing
	a suit fit for space.
As Geoffrey beamed bright,
	with a smile on his face.

"Please take me up, way past the sky and beyond.
Where shooting-star wishes are heard and respond!"

"The sky is no limit, my tall spotty friend.
Please join in my travels. Up to space, let's ascend!"

Despite being night-time, the pathway was clear.
They travelled through darkness without any fear.
To the edge of the Earth, the companions they sped,
to fill Geoffrey's heart. Then the pilot, he said:

"Good luck to you Geoffrey,
find what you desire.
Good luck to you Geoffrey.
Have strength and don't tire.

Feel happy up high;
may your darkness have light.
Feel happy exploring,
with stars shining bright."

Then a voice from the stars,
that shimmered with glee,
Spoke to Geoffrey so clearly:

"Sail oceans with me."

Geoffrey's heart felt a little more full.
Now, slowly he sensed a draw and a pull.

He took a deep breath, towards salt-filled air,
When the biggest of vessels made him stop still and stare.

In dock, was the biggest ship he'd ever seen.
A ship so impressive, it was fit for a queen.

The captain stepped up on the deck with such pride.
"Come join us dear Geoffrey. Please come for a ride."

The vessel was huge; it was big, it was grand.
It even had runways where jet planes could land.
They travelled together, on ocean and sea.
Geoffrey's heart now as full as can be.

"I'm glad that you joined us, my lovely new friend.
Please promise our friendship will not see an end."

"Bon Voyage to you Geoffrey. I wish you the best.
Bon Voyage to you Geoffrey. Have vigour and zest.
Find joy on your travels and don't miss a thing.
Find joy on your journey and make your heart sing."

Then a voice on the waves, coming up from
the sea, spoke to Geoffrey directly:

"Come cloud-gaze, with me."

An inner-peace came as Geoffrey cloud-gazed.
Loneliness fading; now alone, but unfazed.

Away in the distance, he
heard a faint rumble.
So jumped to his feet
with a leap,
then a stumble.

A propeller cut through the white fluffy clouds.
As the rumble got deeper and louder than loud.

Then, a precarious landing of a little old plane,
brought excitement that Geoffrey could never explain.

Without word or warning, he clambered right in,
as the pilot held out hat and goggles for him.

They took to the sky and flew 'round all day long;
and Geoffrey now felt that he really belonged.

The smell in the air and the humming beneath,
gave a feeling of freedom he could not believe.
This plane brought a message of hope from above;
and the pilot shared words of wisdom and love.

"Godspeed to you Geoffrey, new horizons you'll find.
Godspeed on your travels, whatever's behind."

"If you're looking for love, you'll find it inside.
Your strength and your courage should fill you with pride."

Then a voice all around,
now clear as can be,
said:

"Love is a feeling inside, you can't see."

"On your life's journey, away from your home,
just look to the sky, you're never alone."

"Feel the love deep inside,
in your soul, in your heart.
The love that you'll feel,
shows you're never apart."

"You are loved, dear Geoffrey. Take blessings up high."

"Au revoir, see you later, but never goodbye."

Geoffrey, by Louise Conway

Printed in Great Britain
by Amazon

86508018R00025